The Sun That Remembers

Hakim Ibn Adam

DEDICATION

For The Discerning Few Who Seek Truth Beyond The
Obvious, Whose Understanding Is Forged In The Quiet
Fires Of Introspection—
May Your Curiosity Never Wane,
And Your Journey Be Ever Illuminated.

CONTENTS

ACKNOWLEDGMENTS

This book could not have come into being without the silent companionship of many souls—living and departed—whose thoughts, questions, and dreams whispered through the margins of my reading and the silences of my reflection.

DAWN

LIGHT MEETS AWARENESS

The sun rose that morning with full knowledge that Hakim would never see it rise again.

Its light crept across the lake with unusual deliberation, as if savoring each moment of illumination, before spilling through the windows of the modest cabin where Hakim sat surrounded by his life's accumulation of questions.

Dust motes danced in the golden beams—miniature galaxies swirling above uneven stacks of spine-worn books in religion, science and philosophy that leaned on each other to chronicle humanity's ceaseless longing to understand. He did not yet know what the sun knew, but something stirred in him with recognition, as if every sunrise he had ever witnessed had been preparing him for this one.

Hakim's ancestors, nomads and dreamers, wandered from the Near East to the land of the Nile centuries before his birth. Their blood carried stories older than written word—tales of desert stars that spoke in silver tongues. He, too, had departed west in a journey of discovery, landing in sun-kissed prairies where wheat moved like golden seas, wandering close to snow-capped mountains that scraped the belly of heaven, moving toward vast oceans whose rhythms matched the pulse in his veins. Finally, he settled by this tranquil lake, drawn by something he could not name—a quality of light, perhaps.

He was not old by ordinary reckoning—just over sixty orbits around the sun—but the lines on his face told a different kind of age. Not the decay of time, but the erosion of certainty. Each wrinkle was a question that carved itself into flesh, each gray hair a hypothesis that withered under scrutiny. His eyes, deep-set and perpetually focused on distances others couldn't see, held the particular weariness of one who peered too long into microscopes and emerged wondering if the universe itself might be examining him with equal intensity.

For three decades, he studied cell biology in university laboratories and research hospitals. His specialty was the science of cellular rebellion. He became intimate with the ways cells could forget their origins and multiply without purpose. But between the careful observations and statistical analyses, questions began to creep in. Not scientific questions—those had clear methodologies for pursuit. These were different, more unsettling. The more he understood about the mechanics of life, the less he understood about life itself. How could atoms arrange themselves into awareness? At what point did chemistry become experience? When did information processing become the feeling of wonder at a sunset or grief at a grave?

These questions had driven Hakim to this cabin by the lake. Not in retreat—but a space to think, to observe, to let questions ripen without forcing premature answers. His bookshelf revealed his journey. The bottom shelves held his scientific training: molecular biology texts with, volumes on biochemistry and genetics. The middle shelves showed his expansion: Schrödinger's "What Is Life?", Prigogine's work on dissipative structures, complexity theory, information theory, quantum biology. And the top shelves held his current preoccupations: The Upanishads, Rumi's poetry, Ibn Arabi's "Bezels of Wisdom," Eckhart's sermons, along with contemporary works on consciousness—Chalmers, Nagel, Tononi and Kastrup.

It was not a rejection of science but an expansion beyond its self-imposed borders. Each book was a letter in an extended correspondence with mystery. Each page turned was another step on a spiral staircase that seemed to lead both inward and upward simultaneously.

Hakim rose from his desk where he had been reading since before dawn—a passage from Ibn Arabi about the divine names manifesting through creation. He set the book down carefully, feeling a strange urgency to witness the sunrise.

The path to the lake was worn smooth by his daily pilgrimage. His feet found their way without conscious guidance, leaving his mind free to wander. The air carried autumn's first whisper, a mixture of death and promise that came when summer's green fire began its slow transformation into gold.

He settled onto the weathered granite boulder that had become his morning station. The stone still held yesterday's warmth in its depths while its surface had cooled to match the air—a lesson in how things could be multiple temperatures simultaneously, multiple truths existing in the same space. His body found the familiar depression worn by years of sitting, and he wondered idly if the stone had shaped him or he had shaped the stone, or if perhaps they had shaped each other in some conversation too slow for consciousness to track.

The eastern sky began its daily alchemy. First, the black softened to charcoal, then to ash, then to pearl. Venus still reigned in the lightening sky, but her sovereignty was numbered in minutes. The lake surface lay still as hammered pewter, holding its breath for the day's first wind. Somewhere behind the treeline, a bird offered a tentative note, testing the air's readiness for a song.

This was the moment Hakim treasured most—the pause between night and day, when reality seemed most malleable, most willing to reveal its deeper nature. He had read that many spiritual traditions considered dawn a "thin place," where the veil between worlds grew translucent. His scientific training had initially scoffed at such poetry, but years of observation had taught him that poetry often encoded truths too subtle for prose.

The horizon began to glow with rose and gold, colors that had no names in any human language because they lasted too briefly for words to catch. The temperature shifted by degrees so fine that only skin could read them. His breath became visible in small puffs, each exhalation a visible reminder that he was chemistry in motion, combustion made conscious.

And then the sun's edge breached the horizon. In that instant, everything changed. The light hit Hakim's retinas and triggered the usual cascade of rhodopsin transformations, electrical impulses racing along his optic nerves, visual cortex activation—all the mechanical steps he could diagram from memory. But something else happened too, something his training had no words for. *Time stuttered.* The sun seemed to pause in its rising, as if catching sight of him and recognizing something it had been searching for across cosmic ages. The light took on a quality of weight, of presence, of intent. *It didn't simply illuminate— it knew.*

Hakim's rational mind scrambled for explanations. Stroke? The symptoms didn't fit. Hallucination? But his vision remained crystal clear, arguably clearer than ever before. Every needle on every pine stood out in supernatural detail. Every ripple on the lake's surface seemed to carry meaning in its curves.

His heart began to beat with a rhythm that felt older than his body, as if it were synchronizing with some cosmic percussion that had always been there, waiting for him to hear it. His lungs drew air that tasted of eternity—not the sterile eternity of death but the pregnant eternity of the moment before creation speaks itself into being.

And then came the voice. Not sound—something deeper. Not words—something clearer. It arose from the same place dreams arose, the same depth from which love emerged, the same mystery that transformed chemicals into consciousness. It spoke with the authority of bedrock, the certainty of gravity, the finality of entropy: "*This is the last sunrise.*" The message reverberated through every cell in his body, setting up harmonics in bones and blood.   His scientific mind tried to parse it, compartmentalize it and reduce it to manageable proportions. Last sunrise? Was he dying? About to have a cardiac event? His hand moved instinctively to his chest, but his heartbeat, while strange, was strong. No pain, no numbness, none of the classical signs of immediate mortal danger.

But the voice—if voice it could be called—hadn't spoken of death. Not exactly. It had spoken of completion, of cycles ending and beginning, of something his everyday language had no equipment to process. It was like trying to understand ocean from the perspective of a drop, trying to grasp symphony from the position of a single note.

His legs trembled, and he found himself sliding from the boulder to his knees on the dew-damp earth. Not in submission but in *recognition*. Every sunrise he had ever witnessed—thousands of them—had been preparing him for this one. Every question he had asked had been a thread in a web that was only now revealing its pattern. Every cell he had studied, every book he had read, every night he had lain awake wondering about the nature of awareness—all of it had been approaching this moment with the inevitability of gravity.

The sun continued its rise, but Hakim no longer experienced it as external event. The light seemed to be rising inside him as well, illuminating chambers of consciousness he hadn't known existed. Memories flickered through his awareness—not his personal memories but something older, deeper. Images of caves and firelight, of temples and calculations, of laboratories and equations. As if he were remembering not just his own journey but the journey of consciousness itself as it had explored its own nature through billions of eyes across millennia.

The world around him began to shift. Not dramatically—more like the subtle adjustment of focus that transforms a collection of random dots into a three-dimensional image. The trees were still trees, but they were also something else—expressions of an urge toward light that was both physical and metaphysical. The lake was still water, but it was also mirror, also memory, also the liquid thought of a planet dreaming.

His scientific training didn't rebel against these perceptions but expanded to accommodate them. He thought of quantum mechanics, where observation and phenomenon were inextricably intertwined. Of complexity theory, where simple rules gave rise to infinite expressions. Of information theory, where information and its physical substrate proved inseparable. Perhaps mysticism and mechanism were not opposites but different languages describing the same ineffable process.

The sun climbed higher, and with each degree of arc, Hakim felt layers of assumption peeling away like old paint. The careful categories he had used to organize experience—self and other, mind and matter, sacred and secular—began to reveal themselves as conveniences rather than truths. Useful for navigation but ultimately as provisional as the constellations, patterns imposed on stars that knew nothing of the shapes we traced between them.

A breeze arose from the lake, carrying the scent of pine resin and decay, growth and death intermingled in the endless recycling that was nature's deepest teaching. Hakim breathed it in, feeling his lungs exchange molecules with the world in the most intimate of dances. Where did his body end and the air begin? At what exact point did "outside" become "inside"? The questions that had once seemed philosophical now presented themselves as immediate, practical concerns.

He became aware of his posture—still kneeling on the earth, hands pressed against soil and stone. The granite boulder beside him no longer seemed like furniture but like family, shaped by the same forces that had shaped his bones, subject to the same laws that governed his thoughts. The moisture soaking through his pants knee wasn't separate from the blood in his veins—both were expressions of water's journey through various states and systems, temporary configurations of hydrogen and oxygen exploring the possibilities of form.

Time began to behave strangely. The sun's movement slowed to an imperceptible crawl, yet simultaneously Hakim felt himself experiencing multiple moments at once. He was the child wondering at his first sunset, the young scientist peering through his first microscope, the middle-aged man reading philosophy by lamplight, the present self kneeling by the lake. All these Hakims existed simultaneously, like harmonics of a fundamental tone.

And beneath them all, supporting them like the drone note in a raga, was something that had no name because it preceded naming. It was the awareness that made all the other awarenesses possible, the knowing that knew the knowing. It had been there all along, patient as stone, constant as breath, waiting for him to stop looking elsewhere and recognize what had always been closest.

The message echoed again, not as words but as direct understanding: This sunrise was last because it was first— the first one he was truly present for, truly conscious of. All the others had been preparation, practice, prelude. This was the sunrise seeing itself through eyes it had fashioned from stardust and water for exactly this purpose.

Hakim felt tears on his cheeks but couldn't say whether they were his or the morning dew or the lake itself weeping with recognition. The boundaries that had seemed so clear in the fluorescent light of laboratories were dissolving in this more ancient illumination. He was the observer and the observed, the question and the answer, the seeker and the sought.

As the sun cleared the treeline, its light struck the lake's surface and shattered into millions of diamonds, each one a small sun, each one containing the whole while remaining utterly itself. The metaphor was so perfect it ceased to be metaphor. This was how consciousness worked—one light, infinite reflections, each point containing the whole while manifesting as the particular.

Hakim rose slowly, his knees protesting the prolonged contact with cold ground. But the discomfort felt like communication rather than complaint, his body reminding him that transcendence didn't mean escape from form but full presence within it. He was not having a spiritual experience that divorced him from the physical—he was discovering that the physical had always been spiritual, that matter had always been kin to mind, that the division between them was the first and last illusion.

He stood facing the sun, no longer able to maintain the fiction that he was separate from it. The photons striking his retinas had journeyed eight minutes through the vacuum of space to deliver their message, but their real journey had been far longer—from the first hydrogen fusion in the sun's core, before that from the gravitational collapse of cosmic clouds, before that from the Big Bang itself. He was stardust contemplating stars, the universe becoming conscious of itself through the unlikely miracle of organic chemistry.

The voice spoke again, and this time Hakim recognized it as his own deepest knowing, the part of him that had never forgotten what the rest of him had spent a lifetime trying to remember:

"Dawn is for seeking, dusk for finding. Between them, the seeker becomes the witness."

He understood then that this day would be unlike any other. The sun's arc from dawn to dusk would trace a different kind of journey—one measured not in hours but in recognitions, not through space but through understanding. He would traverse not geography but the ways humans had tried to grasp the ungraspable mystery of their own awareness.

His body would remain here by the lake, but consciousness would spiral through history—through philosophy, science, and mysticism—tracing every thread in the tapestry of humanity's search for itself. And when the sun completed its arc and touched the western horizon, he would finally understand what he had always been looking for: not an answer but a recognition, not a destination but a homecoming.

Hakim walked slowly back to his cabin, each step deliberate and weighted with finality. Inside, he made coffee with deliberate care, watching steam rise like incense, feeling warmth spread through the ceramic mug and into his hands with equal tenderness. He would not write yet—if words came, they would come later, after this quiet receiving was complete.

Outside, the sun continued its ancient arc, and Hakim sat in perfect stillness, no longer watching but participating. The coffee cooled in his hands. The books waited on   their shelves. And somewhere between one breath and the next, the seeker dissolved into the witnessing, as natural and inevitable as light becoming sight.

EARLY MORNING

THE FIRST DREAMERS

As the morning light strengthened, filling his cabin with amber warmth, Hakim felt the first pull of dissolution. It began at the edges of vision, where peripheral awareness meets imagination, where the conscious mind releases its grip to deeper currents. The familiar walls of his study seemed to breathe, expanding and contracting with his own breath, until the distinction between internal and external space became meaningless.

Then came the folding—not of space but of time itself.

The scent hit him first: smoke, animal fat, ochre, sweat, blood and the musk of bodies that had never known soap.

His nostrils flared with recognition that bypassed his personal memory entirely, reaching into cellular   archives written before his species had words for remembering.

The walls dissolved, replaced by stone that flickered with shadow and flame. He was in a cave, but not as visitor—as participant, as one who belonged to this darkness and firelight as completely as he had ever belonged anywhere. The cave walls pulsed with images painted in earth pigments: bison with eyes that seemed to track movement, horses caught mid-gallop, the negative spaces of human hands pressed against stone like signatures on a cosmic contract.

Around the fire sat his tribe—not his ancestors by blood alone but by something deeper. They wore the skins of animals they had thanked before killing, their faces painted with designs that were both decoration and invocation. Their eyes held a quality of attention he recognized from his years of scientific observation, but directed toward different mysteries.

An old woman tended the fire with movements that carried the weight of ritual. Each placement of wood, each stirring of coals followed patterns passed down through generations beyond counting. She was the keeper of more than flame—she was the one who remembered which plants healed and which killed, which stars marked the migration of herds, which songs could call rain or settle the spirits of the dead. Her knowledge lived not in books but in her bones, encoded in gesture and breath.

Beside her, a young man worked flint with patient percussion, each strike calibrated by feel rather than theory. The stone spoke to him through vibration and resistance, revealing its hidden planes of cleavage, its willingness to become tool. He wasn't imposing form on matter—he was conversing with it, finding the spear point that already existed within the stone, waiting to be released.

But it was the painter who drew Hakim's deepest attention. She stood before a section of cave wall where firelight and shadow created a natural canvas. Her fingers were stained with ochre—red as blood, yellow as sun, black as the space between stars. She studied the rock's surface with the intensity of a scientist preparing an experiment, but her purpose was different. She wasn't trying to represent—she was trying to invoke.

When she finally moved, it was with the certainty of one who had received instructions from sources beyond human consultation. Her hand swept across the stone, leaving the outline of a bison's hump. Another movement birthed a horn, then an eye that seemed to open as she drew it. The image emerged not as copy but as capture—she was binding something essential about the bison into the stone, creating a connection that would allow her people to touch the animal's spirit even when the herds were distant.

Hakim understood with a shock of recognition: this was humanity's first technology of consciousness. Not the spear or the fire, revolutionary as those were, but the *ability to take inner experience and give it outer form*. The painting wasn't decoration or even representation—it was a tool for accessing the numinous, for keeping the dialogue between human and more-than-human worlds open and flowing.

The painter stepped back, and others approached the image. They didn't simply look—they participated. An old man placed his palm against the painted bison and closed his eyes, his lips moving in what might have been prayer or conversation. A child traced the outline with one finger, learning through touch what the eyes alone couldn't convey. The image had become a *portal*, a place where the membrane between inner and outer grew permeable.

Language here was different—not the complex symbolic system Hakim knew, but something more immediate, more embodied. They spoke in fluid gestures, in tones that carried meaning below the level of words, in shared silences that communicated more than speech. When they did use what might be called words, these were less labels than invocations—sounds that didn't simply point to things but participated in their essence.

A man returned from hunting, and his arrival sparked a transformation in the cave's atmosphere. He didn't need to announce success or failure—his body told the story in its posture, its rhythm, its scent. The others read him like a text written in flesh and movement. When he began to move in what modern eyes might call dance, he wasn't performing— he was transmitting. His body became the hunt itself, every gesture encoding crucial information about the behavior of prey, the lay of land and the presence of predators.

The others joined him, not in imitation but in expansion. Each body added its own thread to the narrative, weaving a collective understanding that no single perspective could achieve. An elder's movements showed how the herds had moved in other years, a woman's gestures indicated where healing plants grew along the migration route, a youth's energetic leaps suggested new strategies for the kill.

Hakim realized he was witnessing the birth of what would later be called culture, but here it was *inseparable* from nature. These people didn't see themselves as living "in" an environment—they were *participants* in a vast, ongoing conversation where every element had voice and agency. The river spoke through its seasonal changes, the sky through its patterns of cloud and clear, the earth through what it chose to grow or withhold. And humans spoke back, not as masters but as one voice in a cosmic chorus.

Death here wore a different face than in Hakim's world. When an elder lay dying, the tribe gathered not in desperate medical intervention but in accompaniment. They sang the dying one across the threshold, their voices creating a bridge of sound between states of being. The body would be returned to earth or sky with ceremonies that suggested not ending but *transformation*—the same consciousness that had animated the human form dispersing back into the larger awareness from which it had temporarily crystallized.

Hakim watched a child's initiation into deeper mysteries. The boy had reached the age where childhood's unconscious participation must give way to conscious relationship. The shamans—for lack of a better word—prepared him through fasting and isolation, thinning the veils of ordinary perception until he could perceive what was always there but usually ignored.

When they finally led him to a sacred site—a grove where trees grew in a perfect circle, their branches interweaving overhead like neural networks—the boy's eyes held the particular terror and wonder of one about to lose the comfort of smaller identity. The ritual that followed was simultaneously brutal and tender, stripping away the child's ego-boundaries while surrounding him with the tribe's collective support.

They used sacred plants—teachers, they called them—that opened doorways in consciousness. Not for entertainment or escape but for education in the deepest sense. Under their influence, the boy experienced himself as tree, as stream, as hawk, as stone. Not metaphorically but directly, his consciousness expanding beyond the borders of skin to taste what existence felt like from other perspectives. When he returned to ordinary awareness, he carried maps of territory that couldn't be reached by foot alone.

This was education in its original sense—not the filling of an empty vessel but the leading out of innate knowing. The boy learned that consciousness wasn't his private possession but a community resource, a field in which all beings participated according to their nature. His human gift was not superiority but responsibility—the ability to be aware of awareness itself, to serve as witness and voice for the larger dreaming.

Hakim felt tears on his cheeks as he recognized what had been lost. Not the specific practices—those had evolved for good reasons. But the fundamental recognition that consciousness was *ecology*, that awareness existed not in isolated packets but as a field phenomenon in which every being participated. These ancestors hadn't needed to solve the "hard problem of consciousness" because they'd never created it. They lived in a world where inner and outer reflected each other perfectly, where dream and wake were different modes of the same reality, where the human task was not to master but to maintain relationship.

A woman began to sing, and her voice carried the particular quality of truth that transcends language. She sang of the first fire, stolen from the sky-beings by Crow, who paid for the theft with his burned feathers. She sang of the agreement between human and animal, how the prey offered itself to the hunter who approached with proper reverence. She sang of the plants that chose to be medicine, the stones that consented to be tools, the trees that dreamed themselves into shelters.

The fire burned lower, and shadows danced on the cave walls, making the painted animals seem to move with life of their own. Or perhaps they did move—in this state of expanded awareness, Hakim couldn't maintain the rigid distinction between representation and reality that his scientific training insisted upon. The paintings were both symbol and substance, both map and territory, both human creation and independent entity.

He understood now why the first art had been sacred art. These images weren't early attempts at representation that would eventually evolve into photographic realism. They were technologies for maintaining contact with the numinous, for keeping the channels open between human consciousness and the larger awareness in which it swam. Every hand pressed against stone, every animal captured in ochre was a prayer and promise:

We remember.

We maintain the connection.

We hold our place in the greater dreaming.

As dawn strengthened outside where his physical form still sat in the cabin, Hakim felt the cave beginning to fade. But before it dissolved entirely, the old woman by the fire looked directly at him across the millennia. Her eyes held no surprise at his presence—in the fluid time of vision, all moments existed simultaneously. She reached into a leather pouch and withdrew something, holding it out to him with a gesture that was both offering and challenge.

It was a stone, smooth from handling, with natural markings that suggested a face in profile. But as Hakim looked closer, the face shifted—now human, now animal, now something that preceded the division between them. The stone pulsed with warmth that had nothing to do with temperature, carrying within it the accumulated attention of generations who had held it, prayed with it, recognized it as a node where consciousness had crystallized into form.

"*This is the first teaching,*" the woman said without words, her meaning arriving directly in his understanding. "*Before the word, before the thought, before the division—this. The knowing that knows itself through stone and star, flesh and flame. You have forgotten, but the memory lives in your cells. Remember.*"

The cave dissolved, but the warmth of the stone remained in Hakim's palm even as his awareness returned to the cabin. He looked down at his empty hand, still feeling the weight of what had been placed there. Not a physical object but a transmission, a seed of understanding that would unfold as his journey continued.

Outside, the sun climbed higher, its light shifting from golden to white. The lake surface had begun to dance with small waves as the morning breeze arose. A hawk circled overhead, riding thermals that were invisible but undeniably real—a perfect metaphor for the currents of consciousness that supported all awareness while remaining forever beyond direct perception.

Hakim understood that he had been shown the baseline, the original condition from which all human seeking had departed. Those cave dwellers hadn't been primitive—they had been complete, living in full participation with a conscious cosmos. Every development since—agriculture, civilization, science, philosophy—had been an attempt to recapture that completeness through increasingly complex means. But complexity itself had become a barrier, each new system of understanding adding another layer of separation between human consciousness and its ground.

He rose from his chair, muscles stiff from sitting, and walked to the window. The world outside looked the same but felt different, as if he were seeing it through ancient eyes overlaid on his modern perception. Every tree was both botanical specimen and breathing presence. Every bird both product of evolution and messenger from realms that preceded division into physical and metaphysical.

The journey had begun in earnest. The cave painters had known through participation. But participation alone hadn't been enough—consciousness wanted to see itself from new angles, to explore its own depths through the mirror of manifest existence.

That exploration would require leaving the cave, leaving the circle of firelight, leaving the immediate participation for the longer journey through separation and return. It would require the birth of language that divided as well as connected, the rise of agriculture that promised security at the cost of direct relationship, the emergence of cities where humans would forget the stars and remember them and forget them again in endless cycles.

As morning approached its fullness, Hakim felt the next wave of dissolution approaching. The first teaching had been given. The journey into forgetting was about to begin.

MID-MORNING

SEPARATION BECOMES SPEECH

The dissolution came more swiftly this time, as if the barriers between states of consciousness had been permanently thinned. The morning light streaming through his cabin windows took on the quality of hammered gold, and within that light, Hakim felt himself pulled forward through millennia. Through the rise and fall of unnamed civilizations, through the slow discovery of seeds and seasons, through the first walls built to separate inside from outside, sacred from profane, us from them.

When the world reformed around him, he stood in blazing noon heat on a street paved with baked brick. The city rose before him like humanity's answer to mountains—

ziggurats climbing toward heaven in precise mathematical steps, each level a mediation between earth and sky. This was Babylon, not the fallen city of later scripture but the living metropolis at its height, when it was the axis mundi of the known world.

The air shimmered with heat and human ambition. Merchants called their wares in a dozen tongues. Priests in white linen climbed the great ziggurat's steps, carrying offerings of grain and oil to the gods who lived in the high places. Scribes sat in whatever shade they could find, their styluses dancing across wet clay, transforming speech into marks that could outlive the speaker by millennia.

But beneath the commercial bustle and religious pageantry, Hakim sensed a profound shift in consciousness itself. These people no longer lived in the immediate participation he had witnessed in the cave. They had discovered *time*—not the cyclical time of seasons but historical time, time that accumulated, time that could be counted and controlled. They had discovered *law*—not the organic patterns of tribal custom but codified rules that applied regardless of relationship. They had discovered the *self*—not the fluid self that merged with tribe and cosmos but the bounded self that could own property, make contracts and sin against absent gods.

He wandered through the city's quarters, observing how human consciousness had reorganized itself around new possibilities and new anxieties. In the temple complex, he watched priests performing rituals that had been formalized into precise liturgies. Every gesture was prescribed, every word written in sacred texts. The spontaneous invocation of the cave painters had evolved into spiritual technology, reliable and repeatable but more distant from its source.

A young priest explained the cosmic order to a group of initiates, using a clay model of the universe—earth below, heavens above, waters surrounding all. "The gods have withdrawn to their celestial palaces," he intoned. "They no longer walk among us as in the ancient days. We must send our prayers upward through the proper channels, using the correct formulations, at the auspicious times determined by the movement of stars."

Hakim recognized the birth of *mediation*—the idea that divine consciousness was no longer directly accessible but required intermediaries, interpreters, technologies of ascent. The ziggurat itself was such a technology, a human-made mountain allowing priests to climb closer to gods who had retreated to untouchable heights. But each step upward was also a confession of distance, an acknowledgment that the immediate presence known to the cave dwellers had been replaced by hierarchical separation.

In the scribal schools, young boys learned to press wedge-shaped marks into clay, transforming the fluid continuum of speech into discrete units of meaning. Hakim watched one teacher drilling his students in the creation of contracts—so many measures of barley borrowed, to be repaid at such and such interest, with these penalties for default. Language, which had once invoked presence, was becoming a tool for managing absence. Words no longer participated in what they named but stood apart from it, *manipulating* reality through *symbolic* representation rather than direct engagement.

"See how the same mark can mean 'day' or 'sun' or 'brightness' depending on context," the teacher explained, his reed stylus dancing across a practice tablet. "The gods gave us writing so that their words could be preserved without distortion, so that law could be permanent, so that memory could be made solid."

But Hakim saw the shadow side of this gift. Writing created the possibility of lying in new ways, of creating false records, of manipulating memory itself. It froze the living flow of oral tradition into fixed forms that could be owned, hoarded and used as weapons. Most profoundly, it created the illusion that consciousness could be captured in marks, that the ineffable could be made effable through sufficient elaboration of script.

In the marketplace, he observed the birth of abstract value. Sheep were no longer just sheep—they were units of exchange that could be converted into silver, which could be converted into labor, which could be converted into status. The direct reciprocity of gift and counter-gift that had governed the cave dwellers' economy was being replaced by calculated exchange mediated by symbolic tokens. People were learning to think in abstractions, to manipulate mental representations of reality rather than engaging with reality directly.

A merchant showed him clay tokens used for accounting—spheres for measures of grain, cones for small units of oil, complex shapes for more valuable goods. "Before these, we had to trust memory and reputation," the merchant explained. "Now we have proof. Numbers don't lie."

But numbers, Hakim understood, also didn't tell the whole truth. They created a parallel universe of quantity that gradually eclipsed the universe of quality. A thousand sheep represented by marks on clay were not the same as a thousand sheep known individually, with their particular temperaments and histories. The gain in cognitive control came at the cost of intimate knowledge.

It was in the religious quarter that Hakim encountered the figure who would crystallize his understanding of this transition. The man didn't look like a prophet or a priest—his clothes were those of a merchant, his hands stained with the ink of commerce rather than the blood of sacrifice. But his eyes held a quality Hakim recognized from the cave painter, the old woman by the fire—the look of one who had touched something beyond the reach of common sight.

The man sat in the shade of a date palm, surrounded by a small group of listeners—not the wealthy or the powerful but workers, slaves, foreigners, those whom the great machinery of civilization had pushed to its margins. He was telling a story, but it was unlike the official myths proclaimed from temple heights. This was quieter, more intimate, more dangerous.

"In the beginning," he said, his voice carrying the rhythm of one who had learned his tales not from tablets but from desert nights, "there was no beginning. There was only the One, alone with Itself, containing all possibilities but knowing none of them. And the One gazed into the mirror of Its own being and saw... what? Not another, for there was no other. Not Itself, for there was no self to see. It saw the possibility of seeing, the potential for knowledge, the seeds of every story that would ever be told."

The listeners leaned in, recognizing something in these words that the official theologies had forgotten. This wasn't about gods who demanded grain and gold, who grew angry at improper rituals, who played favorites. This was about something more fundamental—the mystery of consciousness itself, knowing itself through the multiplicity of forms.

"And the One breathed," the storyteller continued, "and that breath became wind and word, sky and speech. And the One dreamed, and that dream became earth and all that grows from earth. Not creation from outside, like a potter shaping clay, but creation from within, like a seed unfolding into tree. The One became many not by division but by expression, the way a single light becomes countless colors through a prism."

Hakim felt the hair rise on his arms. Here, in the heart of humanity's first great civilization, was someone trying to recover the participation mystique of the ancestors while acknowledging the irreversible journey into complexity. The storyteller wasn't rejecting the achievements of civilization—law, writing, mathematics and organized religion. He was trying to remember what they were for, what they pointed toward, what they could never quite capture.

"They tell you the gods have withdrawn," the man said, gesturing toward the ziggurat looming over the city. "They tell you that you need priests to speak for you, sacrifices to appease divine anger, proper words in proper order to gain divine favor. But I tell you the secret the priests have forgotten: the Divine never withdrew. It simply hid in plain sight."

A scribe in the crowd objected, "But without law, there is chaos. Without proper worship, the gods send drought and plague. Without distinction between sacred and profane, everything becomes contaminated."

The storyteller smiled with compassion. "I don't say abandon law, but remember what law serves. Don't cease your prayers, but recall who truly hears them. The separation you fear has already occurred—not in the world but in your sight. The holy never left. You did."

The crowd grew uncomfortable. Such words challenged not just religious doctrine but the entire structure of civilization built on separation and hierarchy. If everyone was a temple, what need for priests? If the Divine was equally present in palace and slum, what justified the vast inequalities of urban life? If consciousness was the fundamental ground rather than the exclusive possession of gods and kings, how could the social order maintain itself?

Sensing their unease, the storyteller shifted to a different register. "I don't say tear down the temples. I say remember what they represent. Each ziggurat is humanity's memory of the sacred mountain where heaven touched earth. But the touching hasn't ceased—you've simply stopped noticing. Each ritual recalls the original compact between consciousness and form. But the compact renews itself with every breath, every heartbeat and every moment of awareness."

He stood, preparing to leave, but offered one final teaching. "You know the story of the confusion of tongues, how humanity was scattered for trying to build a tower to heaven? The priests say it was punishment for hubris. But I tell you the deeper meaning: the One became many languages so It could discover how many ways there are to say 'I Am.' The scattering wasn't fall but flowering. Each people, each tongue, each way of knowing reveals another facet of the infinite diamond of consciousness."

As the man walked away, his listeners dispersed, but Hakim saw how his words had planted seeds. Some would dismiss them as the ravings of a mystic. Others would report them to authorities as potential heresy. But a few would carry them in their hearts, would begin to look for the

Divine not just in designated sacred spaces but in the play of light on water, the laughter of children, the mystery of their own awareness.

The vision began to shift, and Hakim found himself moving through time within the same sacred geography. He saw a man leaving Ur, carrying not just his household but a new conception of divinity—not many gods embedded in natural forces but One God. He saw another in Egypt, where the same ancient wisdom was encoded in different symbols, receiving a revelation that would transform tribal deity into universal principle. He saw prophets and sages, each trying to recall humanity to its original recognition while adapting to the increasing complexity of civilized consciousness.

But he also saw the hardening, the institutionalization, the way each fresh revelation became fossilized into dogma. The liberating recognition that consciousness was One became the dividing insistence that only one way of recognizing it was valid. The inclusive mystery became exclusive possession. The pathways meant to lead back to participation became barriers preventing it.

As the vision faded and Hakim's awareness began returning to his cabin by the lake. The sun outside his window had climbed higher, approaching its zenith. The morning's journey through humanity's childhood was nearing its end. Soon, he would be shown how consciousness had tried to know itself through reason, through philosophy, through the systematic doubt that would strip away everything uncertain in search of bedrock truth.

But first, he needed to integrate what he had seen. The cave painters had shown him consciousness in its primordial unity. Babylon had shown him consciousness discovering its capacity for separation and self-reflection. Each stage was necessary, each carried gifts and losses. The question wasn't how to return to the cave—that was neither possible nor desirable. The question was how to carry forward the cave's recognition while embracing civilization's achievements.

The morning was advancing. Next, would come the philosophers, trying to capture the infinite in concepts, to build ladders of logic tall enough to reach heaven. The journey continued, but he was beginning to understand that arrival and departure were the same door seen from different sides. The sun that rose, knowing he would never see it rise again, was the same sun that had always risen, would always rise, in the eternal now where all moments existed simultaneously. He was ready for the next teaching.

LATE MORNING

THE MIRROR OF TWO WORLDS

The late morning sun had taken on a quality of crystalline clarity, each ray seeming to carry not just light but intelligence. Hakim felt the familiar dissolution beginning again, but this time it was gentler, like sinking into warm water that gradually became indistinguishable from his own substance. The boundaries of his cabin flickered and reformed, and he found himself in a garden that seemed to exist at the intersection of earth and heaven.

This was not the wild paradise of the cave painters or the engineered order of Babylon, but something altogether different—a garden built according to the principles of sacred geometry, where every path and fountain, every flowerbed and fruit tree was positioned to reflect cosmic harmonies. The air itself seemed to shimmer with mathematical precision, as if the space were constructed from pure ratios made visible.

At the garden's heart sat a figure in white robes, bent over a manuscript illuminated with diagrams that seemed to move and breathe on the page. His face carried the particular intensity of one who had spent decades pursuing a single question through labyrinths of logic and libraries of learning. Around him lay the accumulated wisdom of centuries—translated Greek philosophy, Hindu mathematics carried on trade routes, Persian mysticism encoded in poetry, all flowing together in this moment when an emerging civilization was the world's great synthesizer of knowledge.

Hakim approached and saw that the manuscript was not one text but many, overlapping and interpenetrating—Aristotle's logic annotated with revealed verses, Platonic geometry expanded through algebraic innovations, medical observations intertwined with metaphysical speculation.

This was the work of a polymath in an age when all knowledge was still one knowledge, before the great dividing that would separate science from philosophy from theology.

"Tell me," the philosopher said, gesturing to a rose blooming nearby, its petals arranged in a perfect spiral, "what do you see?"

Hakim looked carefully. "A rose. Beautiful in its form, pleasant in its fragrance."

"Yes, but look deeper. What do you truly see?"

Hakim let his vision soften, allowing the rose to reveal more of itself. "I see... patterns. Mathematical relationships. The golden ratio in the spiral of petals."

The philosopher smiled. "Deeper still."

And then Hakim saw it—not with his physical eyes but with the organ of perception that the Sufis called the eye of the heart. The rose was not simply exhibiting mathematical properties. It was mathematics made manifest. The ratios and relationships weren't imposed on matter from outside but were the very language through which matter spoke itself into being.

"Now you begin to see," the philosopher said. "Everything reflects. That is the first principle of the true science. The rose reflects beauty—not as a mirror reflects an image but as a child reflects its parent, carrying the essence forward into new expression. It participates in Beauty itself, the divine name "the Beautiful", not by representing it but by being a unique mode of its self-expression."

He gestured to the fountain at the garden's center, where water rose and fell in patterns that seemed to contain all possible movements. "Water reflects the divine name, the Ever-Living, through its constant motion and adaptation. It takes the shape of any container while remaining essentially itself. Is this not how consciousness moves through forms?"

Hakim felt understanding dawn—not the intellectual understanding of concepts but the direct recognition, the tasted knowledge. This philosopher was not merely cataloging correspondences between earthly and heavenly things. He was describing a universe where every phenomenon was a theophany, a self-disclosure of divine attributes through material forms.

"Come," the philosopher said, rising with surprising grace for one who had clearly spent years in contemplation. "Let me show you the observatory."

They walked through the garden, past herbs arranged according to their medicinal properties, past fruit trees whose branches had been trained into living calligraphy spelling out divine names. The path itself was a teaching, moving from the outer courts of sense experience toward the inner sanctum of intellectual vision.

The observatory was a dome of white marble inlaid with lapis lazuli in patterns that mapped the celestial sphere. Instruments of brass and silver stood ready to measure the movements of planets, the angles of stars, the precise moments of eclipse and conjunction. But Hakim sensed these tools served a purpose beyond what would later be called astronomy.

"The moderns will separate science from sacred knowledge," the philosopher said, adjusting an astrolabe with practiced hands. "They will think they honor truth by stripping it of meaning. But we know better. The movements of the spheres are not mere mechanics—they are the cosmic dance of divine names in perpetual conversation."

He pointed to a chart showing the planetary orbits. "Each sphere is governed by an intelligence—not the superstitious star-gods of the ancients but conscious principles that mediate between the One and the many. The moon governs growth and decay, making manifest the divine names, the Giver of Life and the Bringer of Death. The sun reveals, the Light, not as metaphor but as reality—for what is physical light but the sensible manifestation of the Light oflights?"

Hakim studied the charts, seeing in them not the clockwork universe of later centuries but something more organic—a cosmos that was alive at every level, where consciousness wasn't an anomaly but the fundamental substrate expressing itself through infinite forms. The Greek conception of *nous*, divine intellect, had met the revelation of God's signs in nature, producing a vision where every natural phenomenon was both fully itself and fully symbolic of principles beyond itself.

"But here is the crucial recognition," the philosopher continued, leading Hakim to a smaller chamber where mirrors had been arranged in complex patterns. "Stand here, at the center."

Hakim positioned himself where indicated and gasped. The mirrors created an infinity of reflections, each showing him from a different angle, each slightly different yet undeniably the same person. But as he looked deeper, he saw that the reflections weren't simply bouncing light—they were revealing something about the nature of consciousness itself.

"This is the secret of existence," the philosopher whispered. "The One desired to be known, so It created the cosmos as a mirror for Its own infinite qualities. But a simple mirror would show only surface. So It created conscious beings—humans, angels, perhaps others we cannot imagine—as polished mirrors capable of recognizing what they reflect."

"You are not merely material," he continued, his voice taking on the quality of transmission. "Nor are you purely spiritual. You are the isthmus between worlds, the meeting place of heaven and earth. In you, matter becomes capable of contemplation.

Hakim felt vertigo, not of the body but of the self. If he was a mirror for divine self-contemplation, what was the "he" that seemed to be doing the mirroring? The philosopher sensed his question. "This is where logic reaches its limit and another kind of knowing begins. You cannot think your way to this recognition—you must be polished until it reflects itself in you. The rational soul can climb very high through demonstration and argument. But the final recognition comes only through divine self-disclosure to the heart that has been prepared to receive it."

They returned to the garden, where afternoon light was beginning to slant through the leaves, creating patterns of illumination and shadow that seemed to encode meanings just beyond intellectual grasp. The philosopher opened another manuscript, this one filled with geometric proofs.

"Let me show you how the ancients encoded this wisdom. They spoke of emanation—not creation in time but the eternal procession of existence from the One through various levels of being. First the Universal Intellect, containing all forms in pure potentiality. Then the Universal Soul, setting these forms in motion. Then the spheres, then the elements, then the compounds, ascending through minerals, plants, animals, to humans."

He traced the levels with his finger, showing how each stage was both effect of what came before and cause of what came after. "But here's the key insight—this isn't a linear chain but a circle. Humans, through consciousness, can ascend back through all these levels to reunite with their source. The mineral in you remembers its origin. The plant nature in you grows toward light. The animal soul in you seeks and flees. And the rational soul in you can recognize all these as modes of the One Life living itself through infinite forms."

"Is this not heretical?" Hakim found himself asking. "Does this not erase the distinction between Creator and creation?" The philosopher smiled with the patience of one who had faced this question many times. "Only if you think crudely. *The ocean is not the wave, yet the wave is nothing but ocean.* The sun is not its rays, yet the rays are nothing but the sun's light extending itself. The One transcends all forms, while being closer to them than they are to themselves. Both are true, and the tension between them is where consciousness lives."

He pulled out a treatise on optics, showing how he had investigated the behavior of light through experimental methods that would later be called scientific. "Light travels in straight lines, reflects at equal angles, refracts according to precise laws. But what is light? Not just particles or waves but the physical symbol of knowledge itself. When you see, light from the object meets light from your eye—outer and inner illumination joining to create perception. Is this not how all knowledge works? The light of the intellect meeting the intelligible forms of things?"

Hakim marveled at how this thinker wove together what would later be separated into hostile camps. Experimental observation served contemplative insight. Mathematical precision revealed mystical truths. The study of nature was a form of worship, each discovery a new verse in the ongoing revelation of reality.

As the day progressed toward noon, the philosopher led Hakim to one final location—a simple room with whitewashed walls. "All our learning, all our philosophy, all our science—it means nothing if it doesn't polish the mirror of the heart. The Greeks gave us logic, the Indians gave us mathematics, the Persians gave us poetry. But the final teaching is simpler: No reality but Reality."

The garden had taken on the pregnant stillness of noon, when shadows disappear and all things stand in their essential light. The philosopher turned to Hakim with eyes that seemed to see through centuries. "Your age will forget this integral vision. Knowledge will shatter into specialties. The sacred and secular will divorce. Science will explain the how but exile the why. Philosophy will grow abstract, mathematics mechanical, mysticism anti-intellectual. The mirror will break into countless fragments, each reflecting only a portion of the whole."

"But the breaking is also part of the pattern," he continued. "The One becomes many to know Itself through infinite perspectives. Even forgetting serves remembering. Even separation serves union. The spiral path leads away to lead back, descends to ascend, dies to be reborn."

He handed Hakim a small mirror of polished metal. "Keep this—not the object but what it represents. You are consciousness reflecting on itself. Polish yourself through knowledge, through devotion, through service, through contemplation. But remember—the polishing is not to become something you're not. It's to reveal what you've always been."

The vision began to fade, the garden becoming translucent, the philosopher's form dissolving into light. But his final words rang clear: "Ibn Arabi will come after me and speak of the Unity of Being. Others will call it heresy. But you who have tasted, you know—consciousness is not divided though it appears through infinite forms. The sun's light is one whether it illuminates palace or prison. Know yourself, and you know your Lord."

Hakim found himself back in his cabin, the noon sun streaming through windows that now seemed like apertures in a cosmic observatory. His hand tingled with the memory of the mirror, though no physical object remained. He understood that he had been shown consciousness at a crucial juncture—when intellectual sophistication had reached heights that would not be matched for centuries, when science and mysticism still danced together, when the unity of knowledge reflected the Unity of Being.

But already in the philosopher's warnings, he had heard the coming dissolution. The integral vision would fragment. The mirror would shatter. Consciousness would explore what it meant to see itself as fundamentally divided, to experience itself as isolated subjectivity confronting alien objectivity.

He rose and walked to his bookshelf, pulling down his worn copy of Ibn Sina's "Book of Healing." The words that had once seemed abstract now pulsed with lived meaning. The necessary existent was not a logical concept but the immediate reality of awareness itself—that which cannot not be, the am-ness that precedes all qualification. And everything else, including his own sense of separate selfhood, was contingent—possible but not necessary, real but not self-subsistent, waves that existed only in relation to the ocean.

The sun had reached its zenith. The morning's journey through humanity's philosophical childhood was complete. Consciousness had shown itself knowing itself through myth, through revelation, through rational demonstration. But all these were still modes of participation, ways of being included in a meaningful cosmos. The great exclusion was about to begin—the exile of consciousness from its own ground that would make possible both modern science's triumphs and its peculiar blindness.

MIDDAY

MIND DIVIDES FROM MATTER

The zenith sun hung directly overhead, casting no shadows, as if the world had been flattened into two dimensions. This shadowless moment seemed to precipitate the next dissolution, pulling Hakim from the warmth of integrated wisdom into a colder, sharper clarity. The light itself changed quality—from the golden honey of contemplative noon to something more like winter starlight: brilliant but distant, illuminating but not warming.

When the world reformed, he found himself in a small, sparse room dominated by the smell of wood smoke and melting wax. Frost etched patterns on window panes, and beyond them, a European winter gripped the landscape   in iron cold. The year was sometime in the early seventeenth century—Hakim could feel it in the quality of thought itself, poised at a fulcrum between medieval synthesis and modern analysis.

A figure sat hunched at a simple wooden desk, wrapped in a heavy cloak against the chill. Before him lay a piece of honeycomb wax, and he turned it slowly in the candlelight, studying it with the intensity of a man examining the fundamental nature of reality.

The figure was in the midst of the radical doubt that would reshape Western consciousness. He had stripped away every certainty, dismissed the testimony of his senses, questioned the reality of the external world, even entertained the possibility that an evil demon might be deceiving him about the nature of mathematics itself. And yet, in this abyss of skepticism, he had found one thing that couldn't be doubted.

"I think, therefore I am," he murmured in Latin, and Hakim felt the words land like an axe blow on the root of a tree. In that simple statement, the integral cosmos of the Islamic philosophers shattered. No longer was consciousness the unified field in which all phenomena arose. Now it was split—*res cogitans*, the thinking thing, trapped inside the skull, peering out at *res extensa*, the extended thing, the mechanical world of matter in motion.

Hakim watched as he continued his meditation on the wax. 'When cold, it has one set of properties—hardness, shape, color, scent. When I bring it near the flame, all these change. Yet I know it remains the same wax. How? Not through the senses, which show me only changing qualities. Not through imagination, which cannot encompass all possible states of wax. Only through the intellect,   through pure reason, can I grasp the essence that persists through change.

It was brilliant, this isolation of rational thought as the one certainty. But Hakim could see what the philosopher couldn't—the devastating consequences of making thought the ground of being rather than being the ground of thought. By starting from isolated consciousness and trying to reason his way back to the world, he was creating a problem that would haunt philosophy for centuries: how does the ghost in the machine touch the machine?

The room grew colder, as if the philosophical ice age were manifesting physically. He pulled his cloak tighter and continued writing. "The body is a machine, marvellously complex but fully explicable through the laws of motion. Animals are automata, responding to stimuli through hydraulic pressures in their nerves. Even human bodies operate mechanically—only the rational soul, divinely implanted, distinguishes us from clockwork."

Hakim felt a chill deeper than winter. The living cosmos where every level of being participated in consciousness, was being murdered by logic, replaced with a dead mechanism occasionally haunted by isolated minds. The garden where matter and meaning intertwined was becoming a factory floor where blind forces pushed insensate particles according to mathematical laws.

The vision shifted, and Hakim found himself in a grand hall where natural philosophers demonstrated the new worldview. A lecturer stood before an elaborate mechanical model of the solar system—brass arms holding ivory spheres, gears meshing with perfect precision, the whole apparatus moving in elegant clockwork harmony.

"Behold," the lecturer proclaimed, "the cosmos stripped

of superstition! No longer do we need to invoke intelligences moving the spheres, sympathies and antipathies between elements, occult influences and formal causes. Everything reduces to matter in motion, particles pushing particles according to invariant laws. God, the supreme mathematician, has constructed a machine so perfect it requires no further intervention."

The audience—men in powdered wigs and elegant coats—applauded this triumph of reason over mystery. One called out, "But what of consciousness itself? How does matter in motion give rise to thought?"

The lecturer waved dismissively. "A problem for theologians, not natural philosophers. Our task is to map the mechanism. The soul's relation to it is beyond empirical investigation."

And there it was—the great *bifurcation* that would define the modern age. Consciousness was formally exiled from nature, relegated to a supernatural realm that science couldn't touch. The price of mechanical clarity was meaning itself.

The vision accelerated, showing Hakim the consequences cascading through time. The author of Principia describing a universe of forces and vectors where God was needed only as a first cause. Another declaring he had no need of the god hypothesis. The triumph of the mechanical philosophy in explaining everything except the explainer.

He saw laboratories where life itself was being reduced to mechanism. "See how the leg of this dead frog kicks when we apply electrical stimulation," a scientist demonstrated. "Life is nothing but chemical reactions and electrical impulses. Give us sufficient knowledge of the mechanism, and we shall create life from scratch."

But always, in the corner of every materialist triumph, stood the impossible fact of the observer. Who was watching the mechanism? What was the "I" that studied brains, the awareness that mapped matter? The mechanical philosophers had various strategies for ignoring this question—declaring it outside science's scope, reducing it to an emergent property that would eventually be explained, or simply pretending it wasn't there. But the ghost in the machine refused to be exorcised by denial.

Hakim found himself in another scene—a salon where the implications of mechanism were being worked out for human society. "If humans are machines," a philosophe argued, "then society can be engineered like any mechanism. Find the right laws, the correct arrangements of rewards and punishments, and you can create perfect order. Crime is malfunction. Virtue is proper operation. Freedom is the smooth running of well-oiled gears."

The shadow of this vision stretched forward—Hakim could see it darkening centuries to come. Humans as resources to be optimized. Education as programming. Medicine as repair. Psychology as debugging. The rich, qualitative world of experience progressively reduced to quantities, measurements and manipulable variables.

Yet even as the mechanical worldview triumphed, cracks appeared in its edifice. Hakim watched a young philosopher walking in a garden, troubled by thoughts that wouldn't fit the mechanical mold. "If we are merely matter in motion," he mused, "how can we know truth? For truth implies a relation between thought and reality that mechanism cannot explain. A thought is not true because it's caused by certain brain states—causation and truth are different categories entirely."

And elsewhere, poets and mystics refused the exile of consciousness. Some raged against the 'sleep of reason' that mechanism imposed, seeing it as a kind of deadening enchantment. Others found in nature something that mechanism couldn't capture—'a sense sublime of something far more deeply interfused.' The Romantics insisted that feeling and imagination revealed aspects of reality that reason missed.

But these were rearguard actions against the advancing mechanical tide. The split that had been initiated was widening into an abyss. On one side, the objective world fully describable by mathematics but drained of meaning. On the other, subjective consciousness rich with meaning but severed from causal efficacy. Two worlds that could never meet because the very framework that created them made their meeting impossible.

As noon passed into afternoon, the vision began to fade. Hakim found himself back in his cabin, but the familiar space felt different. He was aware, as never before, of the dualistic assumptions built into the very structure of modern experience. The window that seemed to separate inside from outside. The sense of being a consciousness 'in here' looking at a world 'out there.' The habitual dividing of experience into subjective and objective poles.

He picked up a glass of water and drank slowly, feeling the liquid's coolness, its weight, its wetness. In the mechanical view, this was just H_2O molecules interacting with nerve endings, creating electrochemical signals interpreted by the brain. But the actual experience—the quale of coolness, the satisfaction of thirst, the simple presence of water meeting awareness—where was that in the mechanism? It was nowhere because mechanism had no place for it, could only ignore or explain it away.

Yet he was not simply rejecting mechanism. Its insights were real, its practical power undeniable. The error wasn't in seeing mechanism but in seeing only mechanism. The mistake wasn't in discovering that bodies operated according to physical laws but in forgetting that discovery itself transcended those laws. Consciousness didn't violate mechanism—it included and exceeded it, like a sentence includes and exceeds its grammar.

The afternoon sun slanted through his window, creating patterns of light and shadow that no equation could fully capture—not because equations were false but because they were abstractions, and reality was always richer than any abstraction. The mechanical theatre had shown consciousness one of its own faces—the face that could step back, analyze, manipulate and control. But in falling in love with this face, it had forgotten all the others.

Now the vision would deepen. Having split consciousness from world, human thought would spend centuries trying to repair the breach through reason alone. The Enlightenment was dawning, and with it the magnificent and doomed attempt to make the isolated rational mind the measure of all things.

Hakim prepared himself for the next act in consciousness's self-discovering drama. The ghost in the machine was about to declare itself the only reality worth considering.

AFTERNOON

MATTER DISCOVERS MIND

The afternoon sun had begun its descent toward the western horizon, painting Hakim's cabin in shades of amber and rust. As the light shifted, so did the quality of time itself, accelerating as if consciousness were eager to show him how quickly certainties could crumble, how rapidly worldviews could reshape themselves once set in motion.

The dissolution came swift and sharp, like diving from sunlit surface into deeper currents. When Hakim emerged, he stood on a different shore—windswept, gray, where ancient bones littered the strand like discarded arguments. This was no tropical paradise but a harsh northern coast, where wind and wave had carved truth from stone with patient violence.

A figure crouched among the rocks, notebook in hand, studying something with the total absorption Hakim recognized from his own laboratory years. But this was no indoor scientist—salt spray had weathered his face, his hands were rough from shipboard work, his eyes held depths that came from seeing too much of the world's strangeness.

The young naturalist, though still early in his career, was already marked by the quality that would define him—the ability to look without blinking at evidence that shattered comfortable assumptions. He was examining a fossilized shell embedded in cliff face far above any current tide line, letting the implications settle into his bones before allowing them into his thoughts.

"The earth speaks," he murmured, not to Hakim but to himself, but in a language theology never taught. "These shells lived and died millions of years before Eden. These bones belonged to creatures no ark could hold. Either scripture lies, or it speaks in metaphors so vast we've missed the meaning entirely."

He stood, brushing sand from his trousers, and gazed out at the restless sea. "But if species aren't fixed creations but flowing processes, if forms bleed into one another across deep time, if life itself is a branching experiment with no predetermined outcomes... then what becomes of the soul? What becomes of purpose?"

Hakim felt the vertigo that the naturalist's contemporaries would soon experience. The mechanical universe had been cold but stable—a clock implied a clockmaker, even an absent one. But this new vision was far more unsettling. Life wasn't designed but emerged.

Complexity wasn't planned but accumulated. Consciousness wasn't divinely implanted but... what?

The vision shifted, showing Hakim the cascade of insights that would flow from these careful observations. In laboratories, scientists traced the branching relationships between species, finding common ancestors in deep time. The tree of life revealed itself not as metaphor but as historical fact—all current forms connected through chains of descent and modification stretching back to the first self-replicating molecules.

"We are not fallen angels," a lecturer explained to a shocked audience, "but risen apes. Our nobility comes not from divine decree but from the struggle of countless generations climbing from simplicity toward complexity. Each of us carries in our cells the memory of the primordial ocean. Our very thoughts are shaped by brains evolved for survival on ancient savannas."

Some in the audience were horrified, others exhilarated. One young woman raised her hand: "But if consciousness is merely an adaptation, a survival tool like claws or camouflage, then our deepest experiences—love, beauty, the sense of meaning itself—are they just evolutionary tricks?"

The lecturer paused, clearly struggling with the implications of his own worldview. "Perhaps," he admitted. "Or perhaps consciousness, once emerged, transcends its origins. A cathedral may be built of stones, but it's more than a pile of rocks. So too the mind—evolved from matter but possibly exceeding it."

Hakim watched as the evolutionary revolution rippled outward, transforming every field it touched. Psychology began studying humans as animals with unusually complex behaviors. Sociology examined societies as organisms competing for resources. Even religion was subjected to evolutionary analysis—gods as projections of alpha males, rituals as group bonding mechanisms and afterlife beliefs as denial of mortality's terror.

Yet something strange happened as materialism reached its apparent triumph. The more scientists studied the mechanisms of evolution, the more miraculous the whole process appeared. How did dead molecules organize themselves into self-replicating patterns? How did mere chemistry give rise to the poetry of DNA, storing information across billions of years? How did neural networks generate the unified field of consciousness from their distributed processes?

Hakim found himself in a modern laboratory where these questions pressed with fresh urgency. The scene had jumped forward a century and a half from the naturalist's beach. Now scientists peered not through simple microscopes but through instruments that could visualize individual molecules, trace the firing of single neurons and map the quantum processes in living cells.

"Look at this," a researcher said, displaying a real-time scan of a living brain. "When the subject thinks about moving their hand, we can see the neural preparation beginning several seconds before they report being aware of the intention. Consciousness doesn't initiate action—it ratifies decisions already made by unconscious processes. Free will is an illusion."

But her colleague objected: "You're assuming consciousness equals reportable awareness. What if the neural preparation IS consciousness in action, just below the threshold of reflective self-awareness? What if consciousness operates at many levels, not just the one accessible to verbal report?"

The debate revealed the crisis at materialism's heart. Every attempt to explain consciousness mechanistically ended up assuming consciousness in the explanation. To study the brain required conscious observation. To theorize about evolution required the very intelligence evolution supposedly explained. The explainer could never be fully explained by its own explanations—it was like trying to see one's own eyes directly.

The vision accelerated through the twentieth century's revelations. Quantum mechanics shattering the clockwork universe, revealing reality as fundamentally probabilistic, observer-dependent. Relativity showing space and time as flexible, perspectival. Chaos theory finding complex order emerging from simple rules. Information theory suggesting reality might be computational rather than material at its base.

Each discovery pointed toward the same conclusion: consciousness wasn't an anomaly in an otherwise mechanical universe. It was revealing itself as fundamental, woven into reality's fabric at every level. The universe wasn't just blindly computing—it was observing itself, collapsing possibility into actuality through the act of measurement that consciousness made possible.

Hakim stood in a cutting-edge physics laboratory where researchers grappled with the measurement problem. "When we're not looking," one explained, "particles exist in superposition—all possible states simultaneously. Only when observed do they 'choose' a definite state. But what counts as observation? A human mind? Any recording device? Any interaction with a larger system?" "The equations work perfectly," another added, "but they don't tell us what's happening in reality. They describe our observations, not what exists between observations. It's as if the universe maintains itself in pure potential until consciousness asks a specific question."

The implications were staggering. Far from being a late addition to a mechanical cosmos, consciousness appeared to be the condition for cosmos itself. Not creating reality in some crude idealist sense, but participating in its fundamental processes. Observer and observed, mind and matter, inside and outside—all the dualities that had been crystallized were revealing themselves as aspects of a deeper unity that included both without being reducible to either.

As afternoon deepened toward evening, Hakim's journey through modern revelations culminated in a vision of the present moment—laboratories around the world where consciousness studied itself with unprecedented sophistication. Brain scans revealing the neural correlates of every mental state. Artificial intelligence systems exhibiting behaviors indistinguishable from understanding. Quantum computers exploiting the universe's fundamental information-processing capabilities.

Yet for all this technical mastery, the essential mystery remained untouched. *What is it like to be?* How does matter organized in particular patterns generate—or express, or participate in—the felt experience of being someone? The *hard problem of consciousness* loomed larger than ever, not because science had failed but because its very success had clarified what it couldn't address.

A young neuroscientist sat alone in her laboratory after hours, surrounded by millions of dollars of equipment, contemplating the same questions that had haunted humanity since consciousness first recognized itself. "We've mapped every neuron," she said to the empty room. "We've traced every connection. We can predict with 95% accuracy what someone will think before they think it. But we still can't say why there's something it's like to think. We've explained everything except *experience* itself."

She turned off the lights and sat in darkness, feeling her own awareness—not as brain states or neural patterns but as the immediate fact of being present. In that darkness, all the centuries of investigation collapsed into the simple wonder of existing, of *being aware of being aware.*

The vision faded, returning Hakim to his cabin where late afternoon sun painted everything golden. He sat quietly, integrating what he'd seen. The journey from the naturalist's idea through quantum uncertainty to the current impasse had shown consciousness backed into a corner—but perhaps it was the corner it had always occupied, the irreducible fact from which everything else proceeded.

Science hadn't failed to explain consciousness—it had succeeded in showing why consciousness couldn't be explained in purely objective terms. Every objective description presupposed the subjective describer. Every map assumed a map-reader. Every theory required a theorist. Consciousness wasn't a problem to be solved but the *condition that made problem-solving possible.*

Outside his window, the sun continued its descent, and Hakim knew his journey was approaching its culmination. He had seen consciousness know itself through participation in myth, separate itself in civilization and early religion, seek unity through sacred philosophy, exile itself in mechanism, and rediscover itself in matter's mirror. Now would come the final recognition—not a new revelation but the original recognition that had been present all along, waiting patiently for thought to exhaust itself in seeking what was never absent.

The sun that rose knowing he would never see it rise again drew closer to the horizon, and with it, the moment when all seeking would cease in simple recognition of what had always been present, patiently waiting for consciousness to stop looking elsewhere and recognize its own face in the mirror of existence.

LATE AFTERNOON

CONSCIOUSNESS CONFRONTS ITS SHADOWS

As the sun descended toward the treeline, painting the sky in shades of rose and gold that belonged to no earthly palette, Hakim felt a different kind of stirring. This was not the pull toward another vision but a gathering of all he had witnessed, a convergence of the morning's journey into a present reckoning. The voices, when they came, arose not from outside but from within—crystallizations of his own understanding into distinct perspectives that demanded to be heard.

He remained in his cabin, but the quality of space had changed. The room seemed larger, as if it contained not just furniture and books but entire worldviews circling each other like wary dancers. Three presences made themselves known—not as visible forms but as modes of questioning, each carrying the accumulated weight of traditions he had spent his life navigating.

The first voice spoke with the precision of empirical authority—Hakim understood this was his own scientific training personified, given voice and urgency.

"Let's examine the evidence, Hakim," the voice began, cool and measured. "Every mystical experience you've had today can be induced in the laboratory. Temporal lobe stimulation produces the sense of cosmic unity. Ketamine generates out-of-body experiences. Psilocybin reliably triggers the dissolution of self-boundaries you've been experiencing. We've mapped these states down to specific receptor sites and neural pathways."

The voice continued with relentless logic: "You know the literature. Persinger's God helmet, creating felt presences through magnetic fields. The replication of near-death experiences through hypoxia. The correlation between mystical experiences and temporal lobe epilepsy. How can you claim consciousness is fundamental when a few milligrams of the right chemical can radically alter it? When brain damage can erase it entirely? When anesthetics can switch it off like a light?"

Hakim felt the weight of these challenges. He had read every study the voice cited. "You're right about the correlations," he responded. "But correlation isn't causation. When I tune a radio to different stations, the circuitry changes with each frequency. Does that mean the radio creates the waves it receives? The brain's changes during altered states might be consciousness focusing itself differently, not generating itself from nothing."

"Ah, the transmission theory," the scientific voice replied with a hint of condescension. "Attractive but unfalsifiable. Where's your evidence for consciousness existing independently of brains? Show me awareness without neural substrates. Demonstrate memory without hippocampal storage. Present perception without sensory organs. You can't, because consciousness emerges from complex information integration in biological systems. Period."

Before Hakim could respond, a second voice intervened— his philosophical training given form, carrying centuries of rigorous analysis.

"The empiricist makes a category error," this voice declared. "He assumes consciousness can be studied as an object among objects, forgetting that all objects appear within consciousness. This is the fundamental reflexivity problem—you cannot step outside awareness to study awareness objectively. Every brain scan, every experimental result, every scientific observation occurs within consciousness. How can the contained explain the container?"

The philosophical voice warmed to its theme: "But your position, Hakim, suffers from equal problems. You've had profound experiences today, granted. But what justifies the leap from 'I experienced cosmic consciousness' to 'consciousness is cosmic'? This is the phenomenological fallacy—mistaking the structure of experience for the structure of reality. Perhaps these states reveal only the mind's capacity for self-induced delusion."

"Moreover," the voice continued with surgical precision, "your non-dualism is internally inconsistent. If all is one consciousness, why the appearance of separation? Why the elaborate evolution through time if everything is eternally present? You're multiplying mysteries, not solving them. At least materialism requires only one miracle—the emergence of mind from matter. You require countless miracles—why consciousness limits itself, why it creates suffering, why it forgets its nature."

Hakim recognized the force of these arguments. He had wrestled with them through sleepless nights and library afternoons. "Perhaps consistency itself is a limited tool," he offered. "Logic works wonderfully within defined domains but breaks down at the extremes. Can logic explain why there's something rather than nothing? Can consistency capture the paradox of self-reference? Reality might be trans-logical, including logic but exceeding it."

"Mystical hand-waving," the philosophical voice dismissed. "The moment you abandon logic, you abandon the possibility of shared understanding. You retreat into private experience, indistinguishable from delusion. How convenient that your position places itself beyond rational critique."

Now the third voice emerged, carrying a different kind of authority—his religious heritage speaking through decades of theological study.

"Both of you miss the essential point," this voice intoned with quiet intensity. "The question isn't whether consciousness can be explained by science or philosophy, but whether human consciousness can encompass the Divine. Hakim, your experiences today—powerful as they've been—skirt dangerously close to the ultimate blasphemy: equating the created with the Creator." The theological voice drew upon scripture and tradition: "Yes,

God is closer than your jugular vein. Yes, the mystics speak of the annihilation of the ego in the Divine presence. But they always maintain the essential distinction—the drop may merge with the ocean, but it doesn't become the ocean. You are created, finite, contingent. To claim identity with the Absolute is the very definition of associating with God."

"I'm not claiming identity," Hakim protested. "I'm recognizing participation. The wave isn't the ocean, but it's not other than ocean either. The traditional formulation—'He is not His creation, but His creation is not outside Him'—points to a mystery that transcends simple dualism."

"Mystery, yes," the religious voice agreed, "but a mystery with boundaries. The via negativa tells us what God is not, preventing idolatry. The moment you say consciousness itself is divine, you've made an idol of your own awareness. This is the perennial temptation—to mistake the highest human experience for the Divine itself. It's spiritual pride dressed in philosophical garments."

The three voices began to overlap, creating a symphony of challenge:

"Where's your empirical evidence?" "Where's your logical coherence?" "Where's your theological humility?"

Hakim sat with the cacophony, feeling the weight of each tradition's truth. The scientist was right—consciousness correlated with brain states in ways that couldn't be ignored. The philosopher was right—his position did multiply mysteries without clear resolution. The theologian was right—the temptation to inflate human experience to cosmic proportions was real and dangerous.

Yet as he sat with these challenges, something shifted. The voices were all his own, products of consciousness examining itself. The very fact that he could internalize these perspectives, hold them simultaneously, see truth in each while recognizing their limitations—what was this capacity? It wasn't captured by any of the voices individually.

"You're all correct," he said finally. "And all partial. Science maps consciousness's contents brilliantly but can't account for the mapping itself. Philosophy analyzes concepts precisely but can't touch the pre-conceptual awareness in which concepts arise. Theology preserves necessary humility but can't explain why the Absolute would create something absolutely other than itself."

He continued, feeling his way toward integration: "What if consciousness is neither reducible to brains nor simply identical with the Absolute? What if it's the relational field where finite and infinite meet? Not substance but interface, not thing but process, not noun but verb?"

The scientific voice objected: "Word games. Define your terms operationally or admit you're doing poetry, not investigation."

The philosophical voice added: "Relational to what? You're still assuming consciousness as the field in which relations occur. The circularity remains."

The theological voice warned: "Interface implies two separate domains meeting. You're back to dualism, just with fancier language."

Hakim smiled despite the criticism. "Yes, language fails. It *must* fail. We're trying to speak about that which enables speech. We're trying to think about that which enables thought. Every formulation will be partial because formulation itself is partial. But the failure is instructive—it points beyond itself."

He rose and walked to the window where the late afternoon sun painted the lake in colors that existed nowhere in the spectrum yet were undeniably real. "Look," he said to his invisible interlocutors. "The sun's light on water. Is the gold color in the sun? In the water? In my eyes? In my brain? Or is it in the relationship between all of these, arising only in their meeting?"

"False analogy," the scientific voice insisted. "We can trace the exact pathway from photon to perception."

"Missing the point," the philosophical voice corrected. "He's highlighting the emergent nature of qualities."

"Irrelevant," the theological voice concluded. "Natural beauty reflects divine beauty but isn't identical with it."

The voices continued their debate, but Hakim noticed something: they were becoming less distinct, their boundaries blurring. The scientist was making philosophical arguments. The philosopher was citing empirical studies. The theologian was using logical analysis. The divisions that had seemed absolute were revealing themselves as perspectives within a larger conversation.

"This is what I've been trying to say," Hakim realized aloud. "Consciousness isn't any single perspective but the space in which all perspectives arise. It's not scientific or philosophical or theological—it includes all these modes while transcending each. The unity isn't at the level of content but at the level of context."

The voices grew quiet, not silenced but integrated. Hakim felt them settling—not as antagonists but as complementary lenses, each revealing aspects of a truth too large for any single viewpoint to encompass.

Outside, the sun touched the treeline, and the sky began its evening transformation. But for now, Hakim rested in the productive tension of multiple truths, feeling consciousness know itself through the very debates about its nature.

The ghost in the machine, the transcendental subject, the divine spark—all names for the unnameable, all fingers pointing at the moon of awareness itself. And like the moon, consciousness remained serenely itself regardless of the fingers pointing, the names naming, the theories theorizing.

The three voices had done their work. They had shown that every attempt to capture consciousness in concepts failed—not because consciousness was absent but because it was too present, too immediate, too obvious to be grasped by the very faculties it enabled. The eye could not see itself, but it was not, therefore blind.

The sun continued its descent, and Hakim prepared for the final act of the day's drama. All the philosophy, all the science, all the theology had been preparation for this: the simple recognition of what had always been present, waiting patiently for thought to exhaust itself in seeking what was never missing.

SUNSET

BECOMING WHOLE

The sun hung low on the horizon, a sphere of molten gold preparing for its daily death and transfiguration. The lake had become a mirror of fire, each small wave a tongue of flame speaking in languages older than words. The very air seemed to thicken with significance, as if the universe were holding its breath before some cosmic revelation.

Hakim walked slowly to the shore, his body heavy with the weight of the day's visions, his mind paradoxically empty and full. The voices had quieted, their arguments dissolved not in resolution but in a kind of exhausted peace. He had journeyed through humanity's arc of self-knowing, from the cave painters' participation mystique to the modern mind's reflexive puzzlement. And now, as shadows lengthened and the world prepared for night, he stood where he had begun—but everything was different. Or rather, he was different.

He found his familiar granite boulder, still warm from the day's sun, and settled onto it with the careful movements of age and reverence. The stone received him as it always had, indifferent and intimate, solid and yielding. He placed his palms flat against its surface, feeling the minute crystalline structure, the eons of pressure that had formed it, the patience of geological time that made human seeking seem like the briefest flicker.

The sun touched the horizon, and time seemed to slow, each moment expanding to contain infinities. Hakim's awareness, sharpened by the day's journey, noticed everything: the smell of pine resin and lake water, the sound of small waves lapping stone, the feel of cool air on his skin, the play of light transforming the ordinary world into something almost unbearably beautiful. And then, without warning or fanfare, it happened.

Not a vision this time, not a dissolution into other times and places, but something far simpler and more radical. The seeking stopped. Not through effort or decision, but through a kind of exhaustion so complete it circled back to perfect ease. Like a wave that had traveled across vast oceans, finally reaching shore and releasing its energy in one last surge before settling into stillness. "I" stopped.

Not Hakim—he remained, breathing, feeling, aware. But the "I" that had been seeking, questioning, journeying—that simply ceased. And in its absence, something else became apparent. Had always been apparent, but hidden by the very search for it.

Awareness itself. Not his awareness, not human awareness, not even living awareness. Simply awareness—the field in which all experience arose and passed away. It had no qualities because it was the space in which qualities appeared. It had no location because it was the context for all locations. It had no duration because it contained all time.

Hakim laughed—a quiet sound that seemed to come from the earth itself rather than his throat. How absurd, the whole journey. Consciousness seeking consciousness was like water seeking wetness. The seeker had been the sought. The question had been the answer. The journey out had always been the journey in.

The sun slipped lower, its bottom edge now kissing the horizon. The sky blazed with colors that existed only in this moment, this unrepeatable configuration of light and atmosphere and perceiving. Beautiful, yes, but the beauty wasn't separate from the awareness of it. They arose together, depended on each other, were perhaps different names for the same nameless process.

The scientific voice in him noted that this state correlated with particular brainwave patterns, with decreased activity in the default mode network, with increased gamma wave coherence. All true, all measurable. But like measuring the weight of a poem to understand its meaning. The correlates were real but pointed beyond themselves.

The philosophical voice observed the logical peculiarity of awareness being aware of itself, the strange loop of self-reference that generated paradox. Also true, also partial. Logic could trace the structure but not taste the actuality.

The theological voice whispered of divine presence, of the mysterium tremendum, of the God closer than breath. True again, but incomplete. This was about the sacred as the most intimate fact of existence.

As the sun continued its descent, now half-consumed by the horizon, memories arose unbidden. Not the visions of the morning but personal memories, the texture of a life lived.

He remembered holding his daughters for the first time, feeling a love so intense it seemed to crack open his chest and reorganize everything inside. Where had that love come from? Not from evolutionary imperatives or neurochemical cascades, though these played their roles. It had welled up from some deeper source, as if the universe were loving itself through his temporarily configured form.

He remembered his mother's death and the devastating grief. How her absence had been a presence, how losing her had taught him about the deathless nature of love itself. The form passes but what moved through the form—did that die? Could awareness itself die? Or did it simply withdraw from one configuration to express through others?

These memories arose and passed like clouds across the sky of awareness, each one poignant, each one partial, each one a note in a symphony too vast for any human ear to hear completely. And beneath them all, supporting them like silence supports sound, was the simple fact of being aware, of consciousness knowing itself through the bittersweet beauty of finite experience.

The sun was three-quarters gone now, the sky beginning its transformation from gold to purple. A few early stars appeared, and Hakim smiled at the poetry of it—ancient light reaching his eyes across impossible distances, the past touching the present in an eternal now. Those stars might already be dead, their light outlasting them. Or they might blaze on for billions of years after his consciousness had released this particular form. Either way, in this moment, star and awareness met in the simple miracle of seeing.

The sun kissed the horizon with its last sliver of fire. In moments it would disappear, though Hakim knew this was an illusion—the sun remained constant while the earth turned its face away. How perfect a metaphor for consciousness itself, seeming to arise and set, to be born and die, while remaining eternally present, simply hidden by the turning of attention.

As the final rays painted the sky in impossible purples and roses, Hakim felt his boundaries becoming increasingly theoretical. Where did his body end and the air begin? They exchanged molecules with every breath. Where did his awareness stop and the world start? The seeing and the seen arose together, defined each other, had no existence apart from their relationship.

This wasn't dissolution in any disordered sense. He remained Hakim, seated on granite, watching sunset over lake. But he was also the watching itself, the space in which Hakim and granite and sunset appeared. Both true simultaneously, like wave and ocean, note and symphony, word and silence.

The sun slipped below the horizon, and for a moment the entire sky blazed with afterglow, as if the day were gathering itself for one last statement before yielding to night. And in that moment, Hakim understood the message that had begun his journey.

"This is the last sunrise" hadn't meant his death, though death would come—to this body, to this configuration of consciousness calling itself Hakim. It had meant the death of seeking, the end of the search for what had never been absent. Every sunrise after this would be the first, seen with eyes that no longer looked for consciousness elsewhere but recognized it as the looking itself.

He sat in the gathering darkness, feeling no need to return to his cabin. The stars emerged in their ancient patterns, and he recognized them too as consciousness—not conscious beings but patternings of the same awareness that recognized them. The universe seeing itself, knowing itself, celebrating itself through every possible form and formlessness.

Time passed—minutes or hours, he couldn't tell and didn't care. Linear time was just one way consciousness organized its experience. In another sense, this moment contained all moments, was all moments, each now an aperture through which eternity peered into temporality.

Finally, moved not by decision but by the same mysterious promptings that guide birds in migration, Hakim rose from the boulder. He walked slowly back to his cabin, each step a small teaching in presence. Inside the cabin, he moved with unusual deliberation, as if performing a ritual whose meaning had only now become clear. He lit a single candle, watching the flame spring to life—combustion and consciousness meeting in the simple mystery of light. The room filled with soft shadows that danced and flickered, making the space seem both ancient and newly born.

He sat at his desk where the manuscript lay—pages accumulated over months of writing, his attempt to translate the untranslatable. He picked up his fountain pen and wrote a final entry, his hand steady despite the magnitude of what moved through him:

"Consciousness never dies because it was never born. What I sought in cells and stars, in philosophy and faith, was always here, closer than breath, simpler than simplicity itself. We are not beings having an experience of consciousness. We are consciousness having an experience of being.

To whoever finds these words: look for yourself. Not in books or teachings, though these may help, but in the immediate fact of your own awareness. You are what you seek. The journey ends where it began—in the simple recognition of what you have always been.

The sun sets on one horizon only to rise on another. What seems like ending is transformation. What appears as death is consciousness releasing one form to express through countless others. Do not mourn the wave returning to the ocean. It was never separate. Remember the sun. It never forgets."

AUTHOR'S NOTE

This novelette is not a declaration of new philosophy, nor a claim to original revelation. Rather, it is a contemplative synthesis—one person's journey through inherited wisdom, refracted through the lens of personal insight, poetic imagination, and scientific curiosity. The ideas woven through these pages stand on the shoulders of many: ancient mystics and modern physicists, philosophers and poets, saints and skeptics. Their voices echo here not as citations, but as living presences in the evolving dialogue of consciousness with itself. It is, then, both a meditation and a mirror—offered humbly to those who, like the protagonist, suspect that consciousness is not merely a byproduct of matter, but the very ground from which all things arise. May it serve not as a conclusion, but as an invitation to wonder.